OLIVER LUM

and the

Bubblegum

Written and illustrated by

Jane Preece

Published in UK in July 2021

Copyright © 2021 Jane Preece

ISBN: 9798533200554

This book is dedicated to all the wonderful children that I have taught and read to over the years, particularly my own daughters, Izzy and Maddy.

Thank you to my amazing family and friends, who have inspired me, motivated me and supported me on my storytelling and artistic journey.

All my love

Jane

X

This is the tale of
Oliver Lum,

Whose passion in life
was bubblegum.

Oliver savoured its taste so sweet,

Blowing gum bubbles was truly neat.

His goal in life was to be the best...

Gum blowing champ,

To beat all the rest!

But try as he might,
His bubbles always burst.
His friends' were always better,
So he never came first.

And what's more,
His mother found
his habit
quite foul.

If she saw him
chewing,
She said with a
scowl...

"Oliver Lum, Oliver Lum...
Why must you chew that despicable gum?"

One sunny day, with a gumtastic treat
Popped in his mouth,
As he skipped down the street.

He chewed and he rolled it around his tongue

Sure that today he would not get it wrong.

Oliver puckered up to blow
And out of his mouth a
bubble did grow.

At first it was small, tomato sized,

But as it expanded, he could taste the prize.

Today was different.

Today was great.

He'd boast to his friends,

He could hardly wait!

The bubble grew to the size of a ball.

Oliver could not
believe it at all.

It grew and grew,
Now big and
round...
and WHOOSH...

Oliver's feet lifted off the ground!

As larger and
larger
The bubble grew,
Oliver took to the
air
and flew.

Floating over

rooftops

And gardens below

Eyeballing
with a curious crow.

His mother's words echoed in his ear.

The very same words he would always hear...

"Oliver Lum, Oliver Lum...

Why must you chew that despicable gum?"

He now saw some sense in his mother's complaints,

As his new lofty post left him feeling quite faint.

Oliver's lips were beginning to ache

And he thought in that instant

He'd made a mistake.

He blew further and further
up into the sky.

He dared not look down,

He was soaring so high.

He flew over mountains and deserts of sands.

Forests and icecaps in far distant lands.

There were rivers
And oceans
As blue as could be.
A patchwork world
For Oliver to see.

Then into the inky
black cosmos he rose.
A twinkling galaxy in
front of his nose.

He whizzed 'round the moon
And circled the stars.

At dizzying speed
He zoomed past
Mars.

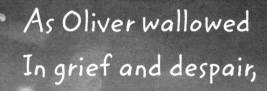

As Oliver wallowed
In grief and despair,

An orbiting satellite
Sliced through the air.

It hurtled towards him.

It could not stop.

Piercing his bubble

With an enormous...

POP!

Gloopy pink gum
Now covered his
face.

And poor Oliver dropped
Like a stone through space.

Down and down and down and down he fell...

Back to the town he knew so well.

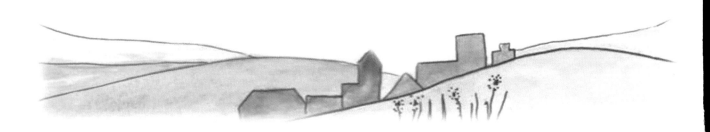

Faster and faster, he fell with a...

Into the welcoming arms of a tree.

Weary and shaking,

Oliver climbed down.

He managed to stumble home through town.

Back home Oliver was a sorry sight.

He looked like he'd been in a terrible fight.

Battered and
bruised,

With a gum
covered head,

His furious
mother
sent him
to bed!

She groaned...

"Oliver Lum, Oliver Lum...

Why must you chew that despicable gum?"

And ever since then he politely declines...

Bubble gum,

Chewing gum

Or sweets of any kind.

From that day on,
Oliver Lum
Will choose an apple, banana,
Or a nice juicy plum.

He learnt his lesson and to this day
He heeds his mother's words and will always say,
"Oliver Lum, Oliver Lum...
Never, ever chew that despicable gum!"

THE END

Printed in Great Britain
by Amazon

86575644R10022